Fun China

Our Chinese Hometown

The Magical Quilt

U0111311

Written by **Ada Ho How-sim**

Illustrated by **Sheung Wong**

Sun Ya Publications (HK) Ltd.
www.sunya.com.hk

Fun China

Our Chinese Hometown: The Magical Quilt

Author
Ada Ho How-sim

Illustrator
Sheung Wong

Reviewer
Judith Malmsbury

Executive Editor
Tracy Wong

Graphic Designer
Karla Lau

Publisher
Sun Ya Publications (HK) Ltd.
18/F, North Point Industrial Building, 499 King's Road, Hong Kong
Tel: (852) 2138 7998 Fax: (852) 2597 4003
Website: https://www.sunya.com.hk
E-mail: marketing@sunya.com.hk

Distributor
SUP Publishing Logistics (HK) Ltd.
16/F, Tsuen Wan Industrial Centre, 220-248 Texaco Road,
Tsuen Wan, N.T., Hong Kong
Tel: (852) 2150 2100 Fax: (852) 2407 3062
E-mail: info@suplogistics.com.hk

Printer
C & C Offset Printing Co., Ltd.
36 Ting Lai Road, Tai Po, N.T., Hong Kong

Edition
First Published in August 2024

ISBN: 978-962-08-8444-3

About the Story

Yan Yan's little brother is about to make his entrance into the world. Everyone in the family wants to send him their blessings. Grandma has sewn all the blessings into a special gift. Read the following story and learn about the gift. Don't forget to send your good wishes to Yan Yan's baby brother too!

As the school day ends, parents and students gather near the school gate.

For Yan Yan, today is a special day. It is not Mummy who comes to pick her up, but Daddy!

"Daddy, when will my baby brother arrive?" With Mummy at the hospital, Yan Yan can't help but ask the same question again and again.

Yan Yan will be a big sister soon. Of course, she is over the moon!

"Soon, very soon! Just a day or two,"
Daddy smiles and replies.

"Doctor, when will my baby come into the world?"
Daddy can't help but ask the same question too.
He is so excited to be a father again.
"Soon, very soon! Just a day or two," the doctor smiles
and replies.

Yan Yan returns home after school.

Usually, Grandma welcomes Yan Yan with open arms, embracing her with love. And there are always treats on the table for her afternoon tea.

But where is Grandma now?

"Whrr, whrr, whrr..." Some whirring sounds come from Grandma's room.

The little baby is to be born soon. Grandma is busy preparing a gift for him with her old sewing machine.

"Hooray! It's finally done!" Grandma announces.

"Come and see. It's so beautiful!" Grandma unfolds
a "magical" handmade baby quilt full of colourful patterns.

"It is a hundred-family quilt*!" Dad gives Grandma
a big thumbs up. "Wow! Mum, you're amazing!"

* It is a Chinese tradition to collect pieces of
fabric from relatives and make a hundred-
family quilt (百家被) for a newborn baby.
The patchwork quilt is "magical" because it
carries hundreds of good wishes from the
whole family, from near and far.

For many months, Grandma worked really hard to make this quilt.

She asked all her relatives for colourful pieces of fabric.
She used her imagination to design the most amazing patterns.

She carefully cut and trimmed the pieces of fabric.

Like magic, she created a quilt filled with love and happy wishes for the new baby.

13

Yan Yan leans closer to Grandma, looking closely at the quilt.

"What a beautiful quilt with rich patterns and bright colours!" She exclaims.

"This piece of fabric is from Po Po*, and that one is from your aunt here in Hong Kong," Grandma explains to Yan Yan as she shows her the quilt.

The Peak Tower, Hong Kong

* "Po Po (婆婆)" is the transliteration of "Grandma from the maternal side" in Cantonese. In Chinese culture, people have different names for their grandmothers depending on whether they are from the maternal side or the paternal side.

Westminster,
London

"Ha ha! These two pieces
came from far away and were sent
to us by plane. They're from your
aunt in England and your uncle in
Beijing." Grandma continues.
"It's been many years
since I last saw them. I miss
them," she says softly.

Temple of Heaven,
Beijing

Yan Yan points to a piece with red hearts and green dots, "It's from my dress!"

She recognises that it is from a dress she wore two years ago.

"You're right!" Grandma gives Yan Yan a kiss.

"My darling Yan Yan is going to be a big sister. You and your brother will grow up together and love each other forever."

In the middle of the quilt, there is a special embroidered piece.

It shows two golden carps jumping out of the water.

Yan Yan suddenly hurries to her room.

She grabs her own quilt and says, "Look, my quilt also has two golden carps!"

"They were sent by your granduncle from Xi'an," Dad says.

"The golden carps are a sign of luck and happiness. Granduncle wishes you to be healthy and happy!" Grandma adds.

Who is Granduncle? Where is Xi'an? Yan Yan has no idea.

Yan Yan puts on her quilt.
    She spreads it out like a pair of
magical wings, as if she were flying high
in the sky.

Tonight, Grandma tells Yan Yan bedtime stories.

"Grandma, where is Xi'an?" Yan Yan asks.

"Xi'an is the place where I was born and grew up," Grandma answers. "It is my hometown."

"Can you tell me stories about Xi'an, please?" Yan Yan asks.

"Sure!" Grandma tucks Yan Yan into bed and begins to tell stories about Xi'an...

23

"The city of Xi'an is one of the birthplaces of ancient Chinese civilisation.

I remember when I was your age we would go see the Big Wild Goose Pagoda*.

Have you heard of the Terracotta Army+? It is in Xi'an too."

* The Big Wild Goose Pagoda (大雁塔) is the place where Tang Sanzang (唐三藏), a Buddhist monk in China, kept the Buddhist sutras he brought back from India, about 1,400 years ago.

+ The Terracotta Army (兵馬俑) is an army of clay soldiers. They were made about 2,200 years ago to protect the first king of China after he died.

24

The stories of Xi'an are interesting yet distant to Yan Yan.

She yawns, and her eyelids start to droop slowly.

A question suddenly crosses Yan Yan's mind, "Grandma, who is Granduncle?"

"He's my younger brother," Grandma replies.

She yawns and asks, "Will my little brother become a granduncle?"

Grandma bursts out laughing, "Yes, absolutely!"

Yan Yan then falls alseep.
Grandma gently kisses her goodnight and says,
"My dear little Yan Yan, one day you will also become
a grandma."

Yan Yan hops onto her magical quilt and flys to the dreamland.

Yan Yan's baby brother is born the next day.

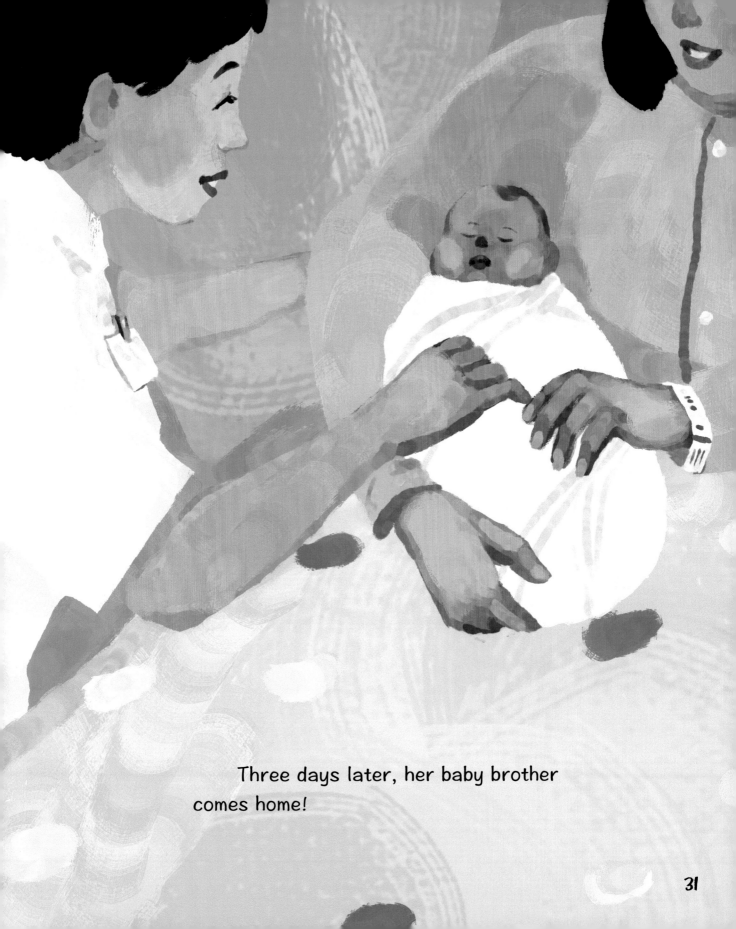

Three days later, her baby brother comes home!

Take a look. Who has the biggest smile in this family photo?

Notes to parents

Sewing a hundred-family quilt for a newborn baby is a Chinese tradition. Elders collect fabrics from relatives to create unique quilts for their babies. This symbolises that the babies will grow up carrying the blessings of their families.

With each stitch using needle and thread, the art of sewing hundred-family quilts has become a traditional handicraft. It shows nostalgia for the old hometown and familial love, representing a close-knit relationship within a family. This practice carries boundless love and blessings that are passed down from generation to generation.

At the end of the book is a suggested activity. Children can draw a family tree to gain a deeper understanding of their own family.

Drawing Your Own Family Tree

In the story, the hundred-family quilt for Yan Yan's baby brother is made from the pieces of fabric sent by relatives, such as her aunts, uncle and granduncle. From the story we know Yan Yan's family has many members. Let's ask the adults in your family to find out more about your family members. Please refer to the diagram below and draw your own family tree on a piece of paper.

Family Tree

Grandpa Grandma Grandpa Grandma

Uncle Aunt Dad Mum Uncle Aunt

Cousin Cousin Me Little brother Little sister

About the Author

Ada Ho How-sim

Ada Ho is an Honorary Fellow of The Education University of Hong Kong. She holds a master's degree in Education from Macquarie University, Australia. She is a former principal and currently works as a writer, school director and guest lecturer at The Education University of Hong Kong.

In addition to her educational roles, Ada has held various public service positions, including school manager positions in different schools. She has also served as a professional consultant on literature and arts for the Leisure and Cultural Services Department of Hong Kong. She was also the former president of the Hong Kong Children's Literature Association.

Ada is committed to promoting children's reading and possesses a profound understanding of and concern for children's growth and development. As of 2024, she has published more than 180 books.

About the Illustrator

Sheung Wong

Sheung Wong is a talented illustrator from Hong Kong. Despite being born deaf, her passion for drawing has been with her since childhood. Graduating with a master's degree in Printmaking from the Guangzhou Academy of Fine Arts, Sheung combines printmaking, and pencil and chalk textures with digital techniques. She has been creating illustrations for various companies and publishers since 2014.